D0535899

HAPPY BIRTHDAY, MRS. MILLIE!

by Judy Cox

illustrated by Joe Mathieu

Marshall Cavendish Children

Marshall Cavendish Corporation
99 White Plains Road
Tarrytown, NY 10591
www.marshallcavendish.us/kids

Library of Congress Cataloging-in-Publication Data

Cox, Judy.
Happy birthday, Mrs. Millie! / by Judy Cox ; illustrated by Joe Mathieu.
— 1st ed.
p. cm.
Summary: Students surprise their beloved but silly teacher with a birthday party,
giving her ample opportunity to make them laugh by mixing up her words.
ISBN 978-0-7614-6126-5 (hardcover) — ISBN 978-0-7614-6127-2 (ebook)
[1. Teachers—Fiction. 2. Schools—Fiction. 3. Birthdays—Fiction. 4.
Parties—Fiction. 5. Humorous stories.] I. Mathieu, Joseph, ill. II. Title.
PZ7.C83835Hap 2012
[E]—dc23
2011016397

The illustrations are rendered in pencil and watercolor on Lanaquarelle paper.

Book design by Virginia Pope
Editor: Margery Cuyler

Printed in Malaysia (T)
First edition

10 9 8 7 6 5 4 3 2 1

Marshall Cavendish
Children

To Naomi
— J.C.

With love to my grandchildren, Alex and Bella
— J.M.

Mrs. Millie is really silly.
Every morning at school she says, "Please hang up your book bugs."
We know what she means—our book bags!

Today is Mrs. Millie's birthday.
She is our very special teacher, so we are giving her a party!
Won't she be surprised?

First, our parents help us decorate the classroom with colorful baboons.

Oh! We mean balloons.

Next, we set out treats.
We have chocolate cupcakes to eat.
We think Mrs. Millie will call them cubcakes.

We have apple moose to drink.
Mrs. Millie will know that's apple juice!

When everything is ready, we turn off the lights and hide behind our desks.

Mrs. Millie comes in after lunch, and we jump up. "Happy birthday, Mrs. Millie!" we shout.

"What a surprise!" says Mrs. Millie. "I'd almost forgotten that today is my bird-day."
"You mean your birthday, Mrs. Millie!" We giggle.

"Look at the foxes tied up with gibbons," Mrs. Millie tells us.

"Don't be silly, Mrs. Millie! You mean the boxes tied up with ribbons," we say.

"Are all these pheasants for me?" asks Mrs. Millie.
"You mean presents!" we shout.

"And look. This wonderful cubcake has a camel on it!" says Mrs. Millie.

"Don't you mean candle?" we ask.

"Blow out the candle and make a fish!" we yell.

Mrs. Millie laughs. "I'd rather make a wish."

We sing "Happy Birthday." We give her cards that we made.

Mrs. Millie opens her presents. She likes the coffee mug. She likes the hand lotion. She likes the new books. Now it's time for games.

"Who wants to play Musical Bears?" she asks.
"Don't be silly, Mrs. Millie! You mean Musical Chairs."

"What a wonderful birthday partridge," she says.
"Silly Mrs. Millie! You mean birthday party."

"Did you plan this all by yourselves?" she asks.
"Well, our parrots helped a little," we say.
"Silly children! You mean your parents," says Mrs. Millie.

We laugh. Mrs. Millie laughs, too.

"I have something for each of you," says Mrs. Millie. She gives us shiny new pencils that read "A present from your creature."

"Silly Mrs. Millie! You mean a present from our teacher."

At the end of the day, Mrs. Millie waves good-bye.
"Thank you for the party," she tells us. "I had a very hoppy day."

"Let's do it again next deer, Mrs. Millie!" we say.